FULL MOON

BY Brian Wilcox and Lawrence David

ILLUSTRATED BY Brian Wilcox

A DOUBLEDAY BOOK FOR YOUNG READERS

For my friends and family
—B.W.

A Doubleday Book for Young Readers
Published by
Random House Children's Books
a division of
Random House, Inc.
1540 Broadway
New York, New York 10036

Visit us on the Web! www.randomhouse.com/kids
Educators and librarians, for a variety of teaching tools, visit us at
www.randomhouse.com/teachers

Library of Congress Cataloging-in-Publication Data
Wilcox, Brian.
    Full moon / by Brian Wilcox and Lawrence David ; illustrated by Brian Wilcox.
        p. cm.
    Summary: A little boy snags the moon with his fishing rod, and it flies him to New York to
visit his grandmother.
    ISBN 0-385-32792-7 (trade)   0-385-90840-7 (lib. bdg.)
    [1. Grandmothers—Fiction.   2. Moon—Fiction.]   I. Wilcox, Brian, ill.   II. Title.
    PZ7.D28232 Fu 2001
    [E]—dc21   00-059034

The text of this book is set in 16-point Sassoon Sans.
Book design by Trish P. Watts
Printed in the United States of America
August 2001
10 9 8 7 6 5 4 3 2 1

For my birthday, Grandma sent me a crystal globe of the city where she lives. "If you look carefully, maybe you can see me," she wrote. I looked, but I couldn't find her.
Before going to bed, I made a wish that I'd get to visit Grandma real soon.

Late that night, I woke to find a full moon glowing in a starry sky.

I whipped back my fishing rod and cast it to the moon. "To Grandma's!" I shouted.

The moon lifted me high, carrying me off to that magical city beyond the mountains, prairies, and rivers.

The city greeted me with swooping roller coasters.
Passengers rode to and fro, shrieking with delight.
"What's happening?" I asked.
But the moon lifted me away before I got an answer.

I sailed over a park where animals roamed and played.
"Are you coming with us?" a giraffe asked.
"Coming where?" I asked.
But the moon lifted me away before I got an answer.

Two enchanted ladies floated and danced over a wide avenue as musicians played a bright tune.

"I'm looking for my grandma," I told them.

One of the ladies waved. "I just saw her strolling by."

"Do you know where she was going?" I asked.

But the moon lifted me away before I got an answer.

Flying cowboys roped faded stars from the sky. One cowboy smiled as I drifted past. "Every star must be polished bright for the party," he said.

"Where's the party?" I asked.

But the moon lifted me away before I got an answer.

Water towers atop tall buildings blasted into the night.
"See you soon," a boy shouted to me.
"When?" I asked. "How soon?"
But the moon lifted me away before I got an answer.

Tightrope walkers balanced on wires between the city's tall buildings. "Time to be off to the party," the elephants cheered.

"What kind of party?" I asked.

But the moon lifted me away before I got an answer.

The moon pulled me past people with fantastic wings.
They soared through the sky like great birds.
"You're almost there," a man told me.
"Almost where?" I asked.
But the moon lifted me away before I got an answer.

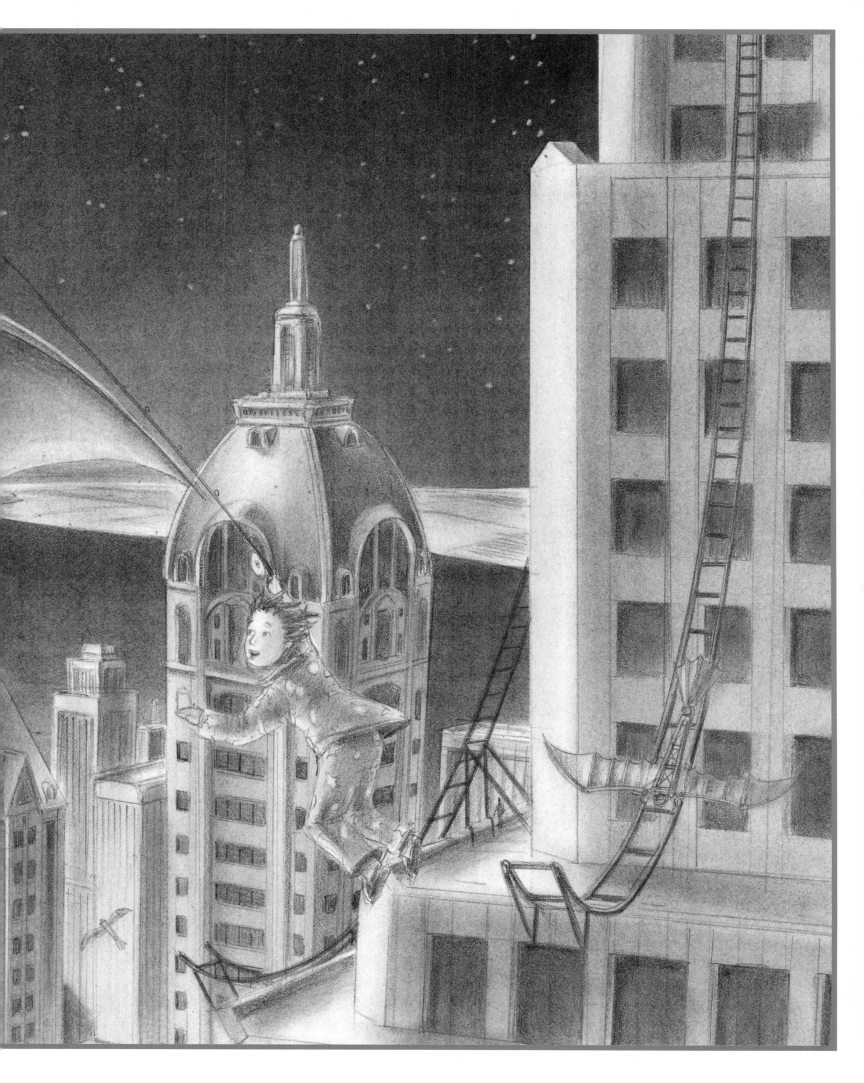

Onward I flew, beyond the big city, down a river, and off to the harbor island, where the great green lady held a torch that lit the night sky.

"Happy birthday!" my new friends cheered. Music played, animals sang, and everyone danced under the stars.

And there, riding on the back of an African elephant, was Grandma.

"Please, Moon, can you stop?" I asked. "Please let's stay for my party."

And the moon stood still in the sky and set me down.

I gave Grandma a hug, a kiss, and a big, wide smile.
I thanked her for the gift.
And the swell party.
Grandma held me tight and kissed the top of my head.
"Happy birthday," she whispered in my ear. "Have a
good night's rest." She gave me a wink and a blink, and
I quickly fell asleep.

Stone lions woke by the library steps and watched as I flew by.

"You're just in time," one called.

"In time for what?" I asked.

But the moon lifted me away before I got an answer.

The next morning I woke in my bed. I took my special gift and gave it a shake. The stars twinkled inside.

And when I carefully peered into that crystal globe, sure enough, there was Grandma riding over the magical city on the back of an African elephant.